"I DON'T LIKE CHOOSE YOUR OWN ADVENTURE® BOOKS. I *LOVE* THEM!" says Jessica Gordon, age ten. And now, kids between the ages of six and nine can choose their own adventures too. Here's what kids have to say about the Skylark Choose Your Own Adventure® books.

"These are my favorite books because you can pick whatever choice you want—and the story is all about you."
—**Katy Alson,** *age 8*

"I love finding out how my story will end."
—**Joss Williams,** *age 9*

"I like all the illustrations!"
—**Savitri Brightfield,** *age 7*

"A six-year-old friend and I have lots of fun making the decisions together."
—**Peggy Marcus** *(adult)*

Bantam Skylark Books in the Choose Your Own
Adventure® Series
Ask your bookseller for the books you have missed

A DAY WITH THE DINOSAURS

BY EDWARD PACKARD

ILLUSTRATED BY RON WING

BANTAM BOOKS
NEW YORK • TORONTO • LONDON • SYDNEY • AUCKLAND

RL 3, 007–009

A DAY WITH THE DINOSAURS
A Bantam Skylark Book / August 1988

*CHOOSE YOUR OWN ADVENTURE® is a registered trademark of
Bantam Books*

Original conception of Edward Packard

*Skylark Books is a registered trademark of Bantam Books, a division
of Bantam Doubleday Dell Publishing Group, Inc.
Registered in U.S. Patent and Trademark Office and elsewhere*

*Interior art by Ron Wing
Cover art by Bill Schmidt*

ISBN 0-553-15612-8

Published simultaneously in the United States and Canada

*Bantam Books are published by Bantam Books, a division of Bantam
Doubleday Dell Publishing Group, Inc. Its trademark, consisting of the
words "Bantam Books" and the portrayal of a rooster, is Registered in
U.S. Patent and Trademark Office and in other countries. Marca Regis-
trada. Bantam Books, 666 Fifth Avenue, New York, New York 10103.*

PRINTED IN THE UNITED STATES OF AMERICA

CW 16 15 14 13 12 11 10 9 8

A DAY WITH
THE DINOSAURS

READ THIS FIRST!!!

Most books are about other people.

This book is about you! What happens to you while you are on a fossil hunt depends upon what you decide to do.

Do not read this book from the first page through to the last. Instead, start on page one and read until you come to your first choice. Decide what you want to do. Then turn to the page shown and see what happens. When you come to the end of a story, go back and start again. Every choice leads to a new adventure.

Be careful! If you make the wrong choice, you may be trapped into spending more than just a *day* with the dinosaurs!

You and some other kids have come to Wyoming for a dinosaur "dig." You're looking for remains of the greatest creatures ever to walk on Earth. Suddenly the leader of your group, Dr. Robert Holmes, shouts, "Here's a strange-looking fossil."

You run to the sandstone ledge where Dr. Holmes is bending over a huge curved bone. He's one of the world's top experts on dinosaurs.

"It looks like a leg bone," one kid says as Dr. Holmes brushes away some sand and pebbles.

As you step closer for a better view, Dr. Holmes looks around. "Would someone go back to the Jeep and get my pick?" he asks. "I need to pry this rock out of the way."

You want to help. But you don't want to miss what happens next.

If you say you'll go to the Jeep, turn to page 3.

If you decide to stay and watch what happens, turn to page 21.

1

On your way back to the Jeep to get the **3** pick, you're in a big hurry. You don't watch where you're going and plunge into a big hole. As you fall, you bang and bruise yourself along the way.

Looking around, you notice that the hole you fell in is actually the entrance to a cave. You peer inside. Your head is spinning. You turn back toward the entrance, only to find yourself in a different world! The ground ahead of you is flat and sandy. Stubby plants are scattered here and there. To one side is a mass of ferns. A low hill rises behind them. In the distance are groves of trees with long, spiked leaves.

Turn to page 31.

4   The head of the brachiosaurus is halfway across the river before the end of its tail slides down the riverbank and into the water. You try to climb higher onto its back, but the slope is too steep. As the dinosaur reaches the opposite shore, its tail reaches the middle of the river. Oh no! Its tail is sinking and you with it!

The water swiftly rises over your head. In you **5** go. The current sweeps you downstream. The river here is wider now—you'll never make it to shore. But suddenly your feet touch a sandbar! Still fighting the current, you manage to wade to shore.

Turn to page 13.

You open your eyes and then blink in the **7** bright sunlight. The egg you found is still cradled in your arms. Dr. Holmes is kneeling beside you and putting a bandage on your knee.

"That was quite a fall you had," he says.

"It was worth it," you say, "to find this egg."

Dr. Holmes smiles. "That's the best dinosaur egg I've ever seen," he says. "We can put it in the museum with the other fossils we've found today."

Your family and friends are excited to see your new dinosaur egg. Everyone wants to hold it.

"Sorry, it's just too valuable," you say. You can hear sounds inside the egg. "Just be patient and watch it," you tell everyone. "Just keep watching . . ."

Turn to page 34.

8   After Dr. Holmes puts Dan gently down on the seat, you take out the bones you found and show them to him.

"These are very unusual bones," Dr. Holmes says as he peers at them through his pocket magnifier.

"What are they? They're too small to be dinosaur bones," you say.

"Size isn't the measure of what's a dinosaur and what is not," Dr. Holmes says as he hands the bones back to you. "Hold these very carefully. Our first business is to get Dan to the doctor. Then we'll come back here, and you can show me where you found them. You may have discovered the *smallest* dinosaur that ever lived!"

The End

As you run, the Tyrannosaurus rex is running too. Each time it puts a foot down, you feel the ground shake. Luckily it's not chasing you. It's spotted a better meal: a small dinosaur called a camptosaurus. It's only three times as big as you are.

On and on you run, through groves of pineapple-shaped plants with bright yellow leaves, past giant green ferns, past the opening to a cave. You hear a screech high overhead. Looking up, you see a creature far bigger than an eagle. You know it's not a dinosaur—none of them could fly. It's the terrifying pterosaur, a huge flying reptile. It swoops toward you!

If you run into the cave, turn to page 19.

If you try to hide among the giant ferns, turn to page 16.

12   Instead, you hear a *thunk*. You lift your head a little. The reptile has just landed a few feet away. Luckily, it has no interest in you. Instead, it pulls a long snakelike reptile out of the ground.

When you see this, you know it's safe to approach the pterosaur. What fun it would be to ride on its back!

Without giving it another thought, you climb on. The pterosaur is too busy enjoying its meal to notice you. Maybe I'd better jump off now, you think. But it's too late! You hold on to the pterosaur's back with all your might as it flaps its great wings . . . and takes off!

Turn to page 52.

Ahead of you is a field of flowers. Brushing **13** aside the tall, feathery stalks, you wade through the field. Big insects buzz like chain saws overhead—dragonflies with wings as long as your arms and bees that are as big as bats.

The flowers smell like wild roses and cinnamon. You breathe deeply. As if a spell had been cast, you instantly fall asleep.

When you wake up you find other kids nearby! Soon you realize you took a nap after lunch. You never did fall into a hole or pass through the Cave of Time. Your day with the dinosaurs seems to have only been a dream. Yet you're quite sure it was real.

The End

"Come on." Tom pulls on your shoulder.
"The entrance is close by."

The triceratops appears once again from
behind some bushes. Slowly it starts coming
toward you.

"That's good," you say. "I'd like to get
home in time for dinner."

Tom looks at you over his shoulder and
starts to run. "We better," he says. "Other-
wise, we're likely to *be* dinner!"

The End

16   You run as fast as you can toward the giant ferns, but the pterosaur circles over your head. It swoops lower. You scrunch down on your hands and knees. You hope that if you keep still, the pterosaur will go away.

Whoosh! You hear its wings beat, and a gust of wind blows by your ears. You want to scream and run, but it is too late now. Any second you expect the pterosaur to dig its claws into your back!

Turn to page 12.

You run into the cave and stop short. In the darkness you can see two huge, glowing eyes. You have entered the lair of another dinosaur.

As your eyes get used to the light, you can see that this dinosaur is no taller than a grown man. It stands on two legs, but its body is tilted forward. It has small front legs, and its head is very small for its body. The danger from this animal is not so much from its jaws but from its feet. One strong kick would be the end of you!

You start to run out of the cave but then stop to think. Maybe you've found another entrance to the Cave of Time. Maybe you've found a way to get home.

If you try to get past the dinosaur, turn to page 25.

If you run from the cave, turn to page 30.

20   "I'm over here," you yell. A moment later you see Tom Ferris, one of the kids who was with you at the dig, running toward you. You brush the red ants quickly off of your legs and stand up.

"Tom, how did you get here?" you yell.

"I fell into a hole looking for you," he says between breaths.

"Do you know how we can get back to the Cave of Time?"

Turn to page 15.

Your friend, Dan Martin, says he'll go to the Jeep.

"Thanks," says Dr. Holmes, as he brushes more pebbles and sand away from the bone.

As Dan runs off, Dr. Holmes looks closely at the bone.

Suddenly, you hear Dan cry from somewhere near the Jeep. Dr. Holmes and the others run after him. You start to follow, but your eye catches something gleaming in the sand. You dig around it and pull out several small bleached bones. One of them fits into the other. They can't be dinosaur bones, you think, they're much too small!

Turn to page 41.

22 On and on you trudge.

Your egg feels heavier as the day wears on. You're hungry and tired. You can't carry it much farther, that's for sure. In fact, you're so tired, you nearly miss seeing a hole in the side of the cliff. Can it be an entrance to the Cave of Time? You're just barely able to fit through the opening. You grope your way along the walls of the cave and step into thin air. . . .

Crash!

Turn to page 7.

You scramble up the huge, rubbery tail. **23** The brachiosaurus starts forward. Its tail moves up off the ground and swings as it walks.

The Tyrannosaurus rex lumbers off in another direction. Fierce and huge as it is, it doesn't dare attack the brachiosaurus.

But your troubles aren't over. If you lose your grip, you could be thrown fifty feet or so with one swing of this monster's tail.

The brachiosaurus lurches to a stop. Its front legs have reached a river. It steps into the water and starts to wade across. You're still perched on the end of its tail. It hasn't reached the water yet, but it will soon, and you don't know whether a dinosaur's tail will float!

If you stay on, turn to page 4.

If you jump off, turn to page 29.

You slink along the wall of the cave. The **25** dinosaur looks at you but doesn't move. It's probably a plant-eater. If it were a meat-eater, you remember, it would have bigger jaws.

Suddenly the beast lets out a *R-O-A-R!* The sound echoes back and forth through the cave. You don't look back. You run—toward a dim light ahead of you.

You're falling. . . .

Turn to page 32.

26 There's something strange about this log, you notice. The front part of it is moving a little from side to side. What's more, the log has stopped drifting downstream and is now moving toward one side of the river! Oh, oh! This is no log. You're on the back of a giant crocodile!

Turn to page 48.

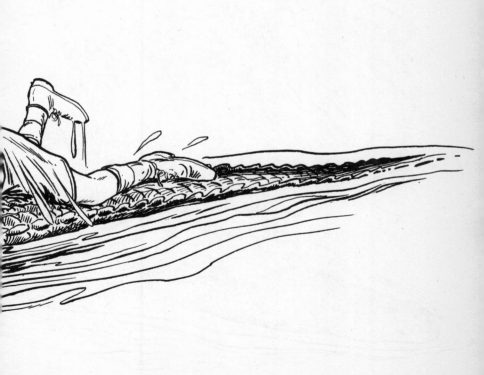

You jump off the tail of the brachiosaurus **29** and watch it wade across the river. You can see the river would be too deep for you to cross: The water almost comes up to the dinosaur's knees.

You walk along the riverbank in the hope of finding an entrance to the Cave of Time. You've gone only a short way when you notice a very odd rock. It's about the size of a football, very smooth, and shaped like an egg. You slip your fingers underneath and gently lift it. It's an egg! If only you could bring it home. Maybe you could hatch a dinosaur. But first you must find the Cave of Time.

Turn to page 22.

30   You run out of the cave and look up at the sky.

Luckily, the pterosaur is gone.

Unfortunately, an allosaurus is standing right behind you.

There is a river near the mouth of the cave. It doesn't look too deep. The allosaurus hasn't seen you yet, but you'll feel safer if you can get across the river.

You start wading. You make it halfway across the river. After that the water gets a lot deeper. Soon it's up to your shoulders. Suddenly the current sweeps you off your feet. You can't make it to shore, but there's a huge log drifting by. You're able to climb on top of it and catch your breath. The only trouble is that the log is drifting downstream toward the ocean.

Turn to page 26.

It doesn't take you long to guess what hap- **31** pened. You've heard about a cave where each passageway leads to a different time. This must be it. The hole you fell into was an entrance to the Cave of Time. You're sure you're not in your own time, because a huge dinosaur—twice as large as a rhinocerous—is walking straight toward you! Along its huge, curving back are triangular plates that quiver as it walks. At the tip of the tail are four giant spikes.

Turn to page 49.

32   You're not hurt.

And you're not in the age of the dinosaurs anymore, either. You're sure of that because a big black dog is barking next to your ear.

Looking around, you see you're lying in some grass near a stream. You've been there before. It's only a short way from the dig site. The moment you stand up, you see Dr. Holmes and some others coming toward you.

"Where were you?" he calls. "We thought we'd never find you!"

"I'm not sure myself," you say, "but I'm glad to be back!"

"We're glad too," Dr. Holmes says. "Too bad you missed seeing the skeleton we found. It's already on its way to the museum."

You just smile: There's no use explaining that you just spent the day with *live* dinosaurs!

The End

34   From time to time you go back to the museum to check on the egg. Weeks have gone by, when suddenly one day . . .

The End

36   Suddenly the crocodile is swimming much faster. It's heading toward a strange-looking animal in the water—a plesiosaur. This one is only a baby—it must have gotten separated from its mother. It's swimming as fast as it can, but you feel sure the crocodile will catch it.

There's only one thing to do! You dive off and swim for the riverbank. As soon as it hears

your splash, the crocodile forgets about the **37** baby plesiosaur. You scramble up on the shore and hear the crocodile's jaws snapping behind you. But you're out of his reach, and the baby plesiosaur got away too!

Turn to page 46.

Ararrrk! A loud moan comes from above. **39** You look up, expecting to see a bird. Instead you see the head of a monster! Your eyes travel down along its long, rubbery neck. What you had thought was a hill is the body of a giant creature—bigger than you thought even dinosaurs could be! The great beast's tail is curled around so the tip is almost touching your foot! Even a brontosaurus wasn't this big. This must be the brachiosaurus, the most gigantic creature that ever walked the Earth. *Garamph!*

Oh no! Another beast is coming closer. It lets out such a roar that you clap your hands to your ears. Coming through the trees is a Tyrannosaurus rex—ten times as tall as you are! It's jaws could kill a lion with one bite!

It sees you.

If you run as fast as you can, turn to page 11.

If you climb on the tail of the brachiosaurus, turn to page 23.

You slip the bones into your backpack and **41** run after the others. They are all standing over Dan, who has fallen into a deep hole. Dr. Holmes is already splinting his leg.

"Dan's leg may be broken," he says. "We'll have to take him back to camp."

He picks up Dan and carries him toward the Jeep. Your friend Erica runs ahead to open the door.

If you show Dr. Holmes the bones you found, turn to page 8.

If you just take them home with you, turn to page 44.

42   You dive into a clump of thick brush and lie there absolutely still. Suddenly, little red ants start marching up your leg. When you can stand it no more, you crawl out into the open terrain. The triceratops is gone, but you jump with surprise. Someone is calling your name!

Turn to page 20.

44   Late that afternoon, you return home from the dig and spread the bones out on your dresser. It looks as if you found a hipbone and two leg bones of a very, very small dinosaur. If only you had the other bones. Then you could fit them together, and you'd know exactly what you've found.

The next day your friend Sam Kendall comes over to your house. You tell him about your trip with Dr. Holmes. "I think I found some bones of a very tiny dinosaur," you tell Sam. "Come take a look."

Sam stands before the table where you set the dinosaur bones. "Did you ever think someone might have had a picnic in the same place you were digging?" he asks.

"Huh?" you say, taken aback.

"You've got three chicken bones here!" Sam says, and starts to laugh.

The End

46   You've learned to be careful. Now that you're safely away from the crocodile, you look all around. Like a hunter you stand absolutely still and hold your breath so you can hear the slightest noise. All is quiet except for the humming of insects and some frogs croaking near the river. Suddenly you feel something brush your foot. You jump with a start, then laugh. It's only a toad! Then you stop laughing in a hurry. Beyond the toad are a pair of huge, open jaws. The crocodile crawled up the bank after you! If it hadn't been for that toad, you wouldn't have seen it!

You don't stop to think about being careful. You run—faster than you ever have in your life—right into the path of a three-horned triceratops!

Turn to page 42.

The pterosaur flies higher still. You feel dizzy and faint. You close your eyes and hang on for dear life. Down the pterosaur comes, landing on a high rock ledge on the face of a cliff. This must be where its nest is, you think. You climb off the back of the pterosaur and settle into its nest to rest for a minute. But the nest is warm and soft, and soon you drift off to sleep.

Turn to page 51.

48   The crocodile is now swimming quite close to the shore. You could dive off its back and try to make it to dry land. The only trouble is that when you dive, you'll make a splash, the crocodile will hear the splash, and then. . .

Turn to page 36.

You run to one side. The creature lumbers **49** by. No need to worry, you think. You've seen pictures of this dinosaur. It's a harmless stegosaurus—a plant-eater.

You watch the animal trod along the sandy earth. It kicks up dust as it walks toward a water hole ringed with bristly plants.

Turn to page 39.

When you awaken, you're still on the rock **51**
ledge, but the pterosaur is gone and there's no
way to climb down. You're trapped without
water or food—only with bones, dozens of
bones stuck hard into the rock. You blink your
eyes as you stare at them. They look like the
bones of the pterosaur you rode on!

A helicopter is whirring around the side of
the mountain! You yell and wave as it moves
closer. You can see Dr. Holmes sitting next to
the pilot. The chopper hovers over your head.
Dr. Holmes lets down a long rope ladder.

"We're glad we found you," he yells down
over the roar of the chopper. "How did you
ever get on this ledge?"

You grab the ladder and start climbing.
"When you look at these bones here, you'll
know," you yell back at him.

The End

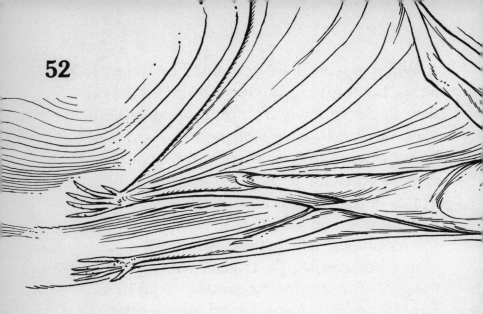

Higher and higher it rises. You stick your
head over the front edge of its wing. Down
below you see the world as it looked a hun-
dred million years ago—sandy plains, shal-
low lakes, fern forests, red-rocked cliffs. . . .

In the distance a volcano spits flames into the sky.

Turn to page 47.

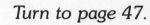

ABOUT THE AUTHOR

EDWARD PACKARD is a graduate of Princeton University and Columbia Law School. He developed the unique storytelling approach used in Choose Your Own Adventure books while thinking up stories for his children, Caroline, Andrea, and Wells.

ABOUT THE ILLUSTRATOR

RON WING is a cartoonist and illustrator who has contributed to many publications. For the past several years he has illustrated the Bantam humor series of Larry Wilde's "Official" joke books. In addition, he has illustrated many books in Bantam's Choose Your Own Adventure series, including *You Are a Millionaire, Skateboard Champion,* and *The Island of Time;* as well as titles in the Skylark Choose Your Own Adventure series, including *Haunted Halloween Party, A Day with the Dinosaurs, Spooky Thanksgiving,* and *You Are Invisible.* Mr. Wing now lives and works in Benton, Pennsylvania.

CHOOSE YOUR OWN ADVENTURE®

SKYLARK EDITIONS

☐ 15744	**Circus #1**	$2.50
☐ 15679	**Haunted House #2**	$2.50
☐ 15680	**Green Slime #6**	$2.50
☐ 15562	**Summer Camp #18**	$2.50
☐ 15732	**Haunted Harbor #33**	$2.50
☐ 15453	**Haunted Halloween Party #37**	$2.50
☐ 15492	**The Great Easter Adventure #40**	$2.50
☐ 15742	**The Movie Mystery #41**	$2.50
☐ 15709	**Home in Time for Christmas #43**	$2.50
☐ 15612	**Day With Dinosaurs #46**	$2.50
☐ 15672	**Spooky Thanksgiving #47**	$2.50
☐ 15685	**You Are Invisible #48**	$2.50
☐ 15696	**Race of the Year #49**	$2.75
☐ 15762	**Stranded! #50**	$2.75
☐ 15776	**You Can Make a Difference: The Story of Martin Luther King, Jr.**	$2.50